Story Time with Signs & Rhymes

Opposites Everywhere
Sign Language for Opposites

by Dawn Babb Prochovnic
illustrated by Stephanie Bauer

Content Consultant:
Lora Heller, MS, MT-BC, LCAT
and Founding Director of Baby Fingers LLC

visit us at www.abdopublishing.com

For Stephanie Hedlund, who patiently helps me navigate the ins and outs of publishing—DP
For my favorite opposites, Izzi and Madison!—SB

Printed in the United States of America, North Mankato, Minnesota.
102011
012012
 This book contains at least 10% recycled materials.

Written by Dawn Babb Prochovnic
Illustrations by Stephanie Bauer
Edited by Stephanie Hedlund and Rochelle Baltzer
Cover and interior layout and design by Neil Klinepier

Story Time with Signs & Rhymes provides an introduction to ASL vocabulary through stories that are written and structured in English. ASL is a separate language with its own structure. Just as there are personal and regional variations in spoken and written languages, there are similar variations in sign language.

Library of Congress Cataloging-in-Publication Data
Prochovnic, Dawn Babb.
  Opposites everywhere : sign language for opposites / by Dawn Babb Prochovnic ; illustrated by Stephanie Bauer.
    p. cm. -- (Story time with signs & rhymes)
  Summary: Playful images and simple rhymes introduce the American Sign Language signs for things and concepts that are opposites: for instance, big/small and smooth/rough.
  ISBN 978-1-61641-839-7
  1. American Sign Language--Juvenile fiction. 2. Stories in rhyme. 3. Polarity--Juvenile fiction. [1. English language--Synonyms and antonyms--Fiction. 2. Sign language. 3. Stories in rhyme.] I. Bauer, Stephanie, ill. II. Title. III. Series: Story time with signs & rhymes.
  PZ10.4.P76Op 2012
  [E]--dc23
                          2011027073

Alphabet Handshapes

American Sign Language (ASL) is a visual language that uses handshapes, movements, and facial expressions. Sometimes people spell English words by making the handshape for each letter in the word they want to sign. This is called fingerspelling. The pictures below show the handshapes for each letter in the manual alphabet.

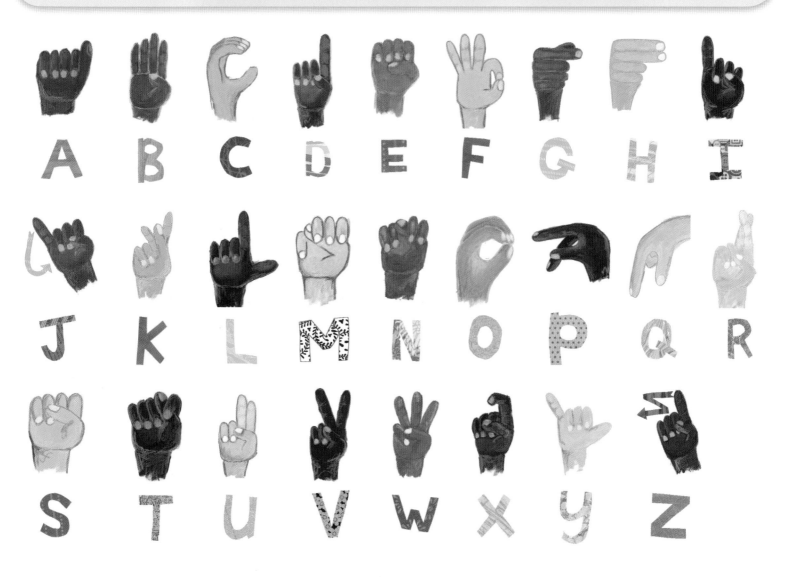

Opposites here. Opposites there.
I see opposites everywhere.

4

opposite

A small, white mouse squeaks.

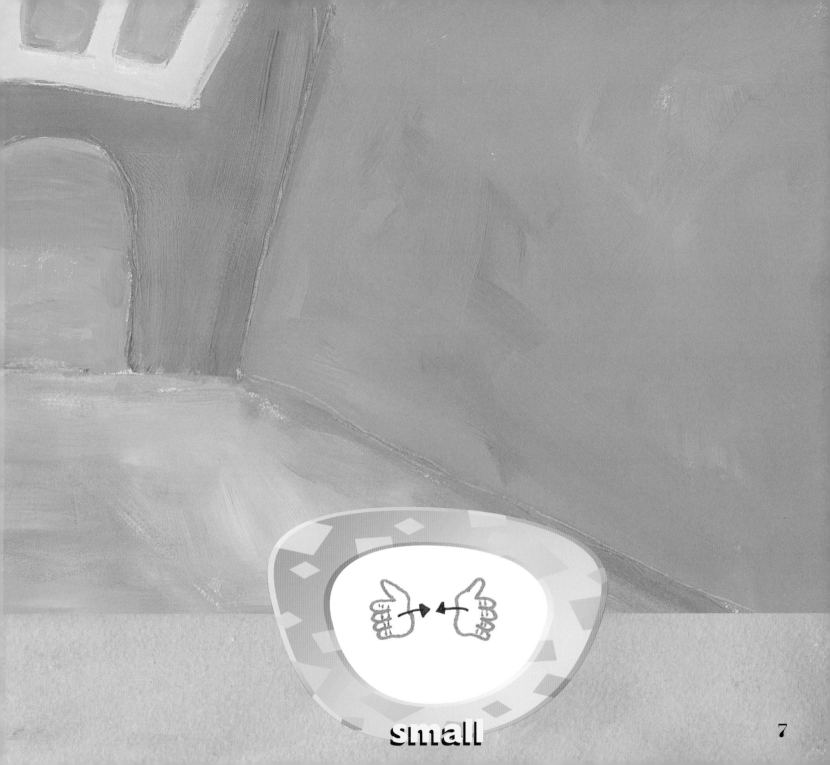

small

The **big**, blue house creaks.

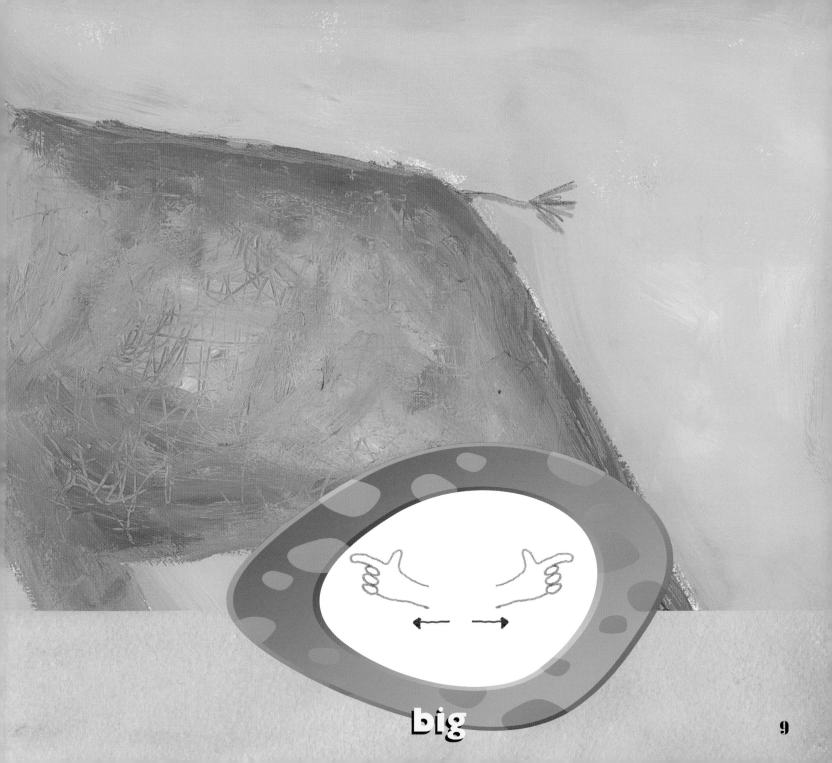

big

The **smooth**, black blocks crash.

smooth

The **rough,** red rocks splash.

rough

The **old**, brown trike rides.

old

The **new**, yellow bike glides.

new

The **sweet**, pink gum pops.

sweet

The **sour**, purple plum drops.

sour

A slow, gray slug slimes.

slow

A fast, green bug climbs.

fast

Opposites here. Opposites there.
I see opposites everywhere.

opposite

American Sign Language Glossary

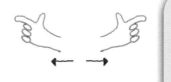 **big:** Hold your "L Hands" in front of your body with your pointer fingers slightly bent and the bent knuckles of your last three fingers pointing forward. Your palms should be close together and facing each other, and your thumbs should be pointing up. Now move the palms of your hands apart. It should look like you are showing the width of something big.

 **fast:** Hold your "L Hands" in front of you with your palms facing each other and the tips of your pointer fingers facing out. Now quickly pull your hands toward your body as you bend your pointer fingers into "X Hands."

 **new:** Hold your left hand in front of you with your palm facing up. Now quickly brush the back of your curved, right hand across the palm of your left hand, starting at your fingertips and moving toward your wrist.

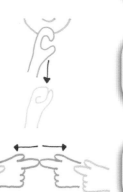 **old:** Make a "C Hand" near your chin. Now move your hand down and close it into an "S Hand." It should look like you are gently pulling on the long beard that is growing on an old man's chin.

opposite: Touch the tips of your pointer fingers together with your palms facing toward you. Now move your hands apart. It should look like your fingers are magnets repelling in opposite directions.

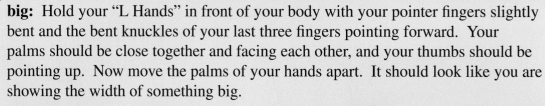

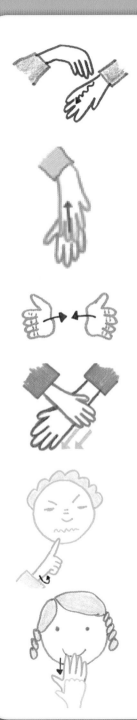

rough: Hold your left hand in front of you with your palm facing up. Bend the fingers of your right hand and touch them to the palm of your left hand near your wrist. Now move the fingertips of your right hand in a wiggly motion across the palm of your left hand toward your fingertips. It should look like you are scratching something that is rough.

slow: Hold your hands in front of you with the right hand on top of the left and both of your palms facing down. Your fingertips should point forward. Now slowly move the palm of your right hand across the back of your left hand, moving from the fingertips to the wrist of the left hand. It should look like something is moving slowly across the back of your left hand.

small: Hold your hands in front of your body with your fingertips facing out and your palms facing each other, with some space between them. Now move the palms of your hands closer together. It should look like you are showing the width of something small.

smooth: Hold your left hand in front of your body with your palm facing down. Now gently slide the palm of your right hand across the back of your left hand, starting at your wrist and moving toward your fingertips. It should look like you are showing the smooth surface of the back of your hand.

sour: Squint your eyes and wrinkle your nose as you touch your pointer finger to your chin and quickly twist your hand so your palm faces in. It should look like you have just eaten something sour.

sweet: Touch your fingertips to your chin then bend your fingers so they touch the palm of your hand. Repeat this a couple of times. It should look like you are licking something sweet off of your fingers.

Fun Facts about ASL

Most sign language dictionaries describe how a sign looks for a right-handed signer. If you are left-handed, you would modify the instructions so the signs feel more comfortable to you. For example, to sign *smooth*, a left-handed signer would move the palm of the left hand across the back of the right hand.

Facial expressions and body language are an important part of communicating in sign language. For example, if you exaggerate the sign for *big* by moving your hands farther apart than usual, you are communicating that something is *very big*.

Words that are spoken or written in English are not always needed when you communicate in sign language. For example, if you want to communicate that someone is *walking slowly*, you do not necessarily need to sign *walk* and *slow*. Many signers would simply sign *walk*, by moving their hands up and down in front of them in an alternating step-like motion, more slowly than usual.

Signing Activities

Opposites Attract: This is a fun game for partners. Get 10 blank index cards. Write one word from the glossary on the front of each card, skipping the word *opposite*. Leave the back of each card blank. Shuffle the cards and put them facedown in a pile. The player who goes first takes a card from the pile and makes the sign for the word on the card. The partner must repeat this sign and make the sign for the opposite word. For example, if the word written on the first card is *fast*, the first player must make the sign for *fast* and the partner must make the sign for *fast* and *slow*. Now switch roles. Continue taking turns until all the cards have been used at least once.

Sign Language Concentration: This is a fun game for partners. Use the index cards from the first activity, and make another set just like it. Shuffle the 20 cards and lay them all facedown in a pattern of columns and rows in front of you. The first player turns over two cards. If the cards shown are opposites, that player must make the signs for both words shown on the cards. If the player makes the correct signs, he or she gets to keep the cards. If the cards are not opposites, or the player cannot make the correct signs, both cards should be turned back over, and it is the next player's turn. Play continues until all the cards are matched with an opposite. The player with the most cards wins.

Additional Resources

Further Reading

Coleman, Rachel. *Once Upon a Time* (Signing Time DVD, Series 2, Volume 11). Two Little Hands Productions, 2008.

Edge, Nellie. *ABC Phonics: Sing, Sign, and Read!* Northlight Communications, 2010.

Heller, Lora. *Sign Language for Kids*. Sterling, 2004.

Valli, Clayton. *The Gallaudet Dictionary of American Sign Language*. Gallaudet University Press, 2005.

Web Sites

To learn more about ASL, visit ABDO Group online at **www.abdopublishing.com**. Web sites about ASL are featured on our Book Links page. These links are routinely monitored and updated to provide the most current information available.